SPECIAL THANKS TO ANNE MARIE RYAN

ORCHARD BOOKS
Carmelite House
50 Victoria Embankment
London EC4Y 0DZ

First published by Orchard Books in 2017

THE POWERPUFF GIRLS, CARTOON NETWORK,
the logos, and all related characters and elements are trademarks of
and © Cartoon Network (s17).

A CIP catalogue record for this book is available
from the British Library.

ISBN 978 1 40834 737 9

1 3 5 7 9 10 8 6 4 2

Printed in Great Britain

Orchard Books
An imprint of Hachette Children's Group
Part of The Watts Publishing Group Limited
An Hachette UK Company
www.hachette.co.uk

the POWERPUFF GIRLS ™

HERO TO ZERO

ORCHARD

MEET THE POWERPUFF GIRLS!

BLOSSOM

Favourite colour: Pink
Aura power: Sponge, broom, stapler
Likes: Organising, stationery, science, punching baddies and doing well at school
Dislikes: Mess, being disorganised
Most likely to say: "Let's go save the day!"

BUBBLES

Favourite colour: Blue
Likes: Animals, creating computer games, make-up, punching baddies, singing, her toy octopus, Octi
Dislikes: Animals being upset, dressing up in ugly clothes
Most likely to say: "I love piggies!"

BUTTERCUP

Favourite colour: Green
Aura power: Rocket, tank, submarine, cannon
Likes: Roller derby, fighting, deathball
Dislikes: Dressing up, wussy people
Most likely to say: "Don't call me princess!"

THE PROFESSOR: The Powerpuff Girls' father, the Professor, was trying to create the perfect little girls out of sugar and spice and all things nice. But when he accidentally added Chemical X to the mix, he got three super cute and super fierce crime-fighting superheroes: The Powerpuff Girls!
Likes: Science, The Powerpuff Girls, creating new inventions in his lab under the house
Dislikes: When things explode
Most likely to say: "How could you hate science?"

PRINCESS MORBUCKS: Super-rich Princess Morbucks wants to be one of The Powerpuff Girls – the only one!
Likes: Money. Lots and lots of money
Dislikes: The Powerpuff Girls!
Most likely to say: "It's nice to be nice, but it's great to be rich!"

THE NARRATOR:

Ahem, and there's me. I'm your friendly narrator. I'll pop up now and again to give you all the gossip on what's going on. Are you sitting comfortably? No? Well then get ready! Honestly, do I have to do everything around here? The book's about to begin! Ready? Then let's go!

CONTENTS

SPECIAL DELIVERY

Some jobs are harder than others. Doctors, police officers, firefighters and writers work tirelessly to keep us safe. (OK, maybe not writers). But no one works harder than superheroes!

"I am soooooooo tired!" said Buttercup, flying into the bedroom she shared with her sisters. She dropped her school bag on the

floor. "Budge over, Bloss," she said, dive-bombing on to the bed next to Blossom and Bubbles.

"Sorry," groaned Blossom. "I can't move a muscle."

"I'm so tired I can't even blink," said Bubbles, staring up at the bedroom ceiling with her big blue eyes.

"It's been such a busy week," said Blossom. "We rescued the Mayor from that gang of evil amoebas, we stopped a criminal mastermind from stealing Townsville's gold and then we fought off an army of mole men."

"Don't forget the out-of-control robot we took down," Buttercup reminded her. She rubbed her shoulder. It was still sore from punching the giant metal menace!

"Or that dragon monster we defeated," said Bubbles. "If it hadn't been for us he'd have burned down the whole town!"

"Sometimes I wish we weren't the only superheroes in Townsville," Buttercup said, sighing wearily.

"Maybe I'll just have a little nap," said Bubbles, cuddling her purple octopus toy.

"We can't take a nap," Blossom mumbled sleepily. "We've still got tons of homework to do …"

That's right — superheroes have to do homework, too! The next time you complain about learning your times tables, count yourself lucky that you don't have to fight crime as well!

"I really need to catch some ZZZs," said Buttercup, yawning.

Her sisters didn't reply, because they had already nodded off.

But just as Buttercup's eyes shut, Professor Utonium called up the stairs. "Girls! There's post for you."

"Maybe it's a new stationery catalogue!" said Blossom, flying down the stairs in a blaze of pink light. She couldn't wait to browse through pages of highlighters, paper clips and notepads.

"I bet it's a letter from the panda I adopted," said Bubbles happily, trailing blue light as she zoomed after her sister.

"Dude, you know the panda isn't writing those letters, right?" said Buttercup, rolling her eyes. "Besides, I'm expecting this month's edition of *Roller Derby Enthusiast* magazine." She strapped on her skates then zipped downstairs in a flash of green light.

Apparently The Powerpuff Girls did have a tiny bit of energy left, after all.

Professor Utonium handed them a brochure that had come in the post.

"*Villageton – A Greener Place to Live,*" said Blossom, reading the title out loud. The girls flipped through the brochure, which had glossy photographs of the neighbouring town.

"I came all the way downstairs for this?" complained Buttercup.

"Oops, sorry," said Professor Utonium, taking an envelope out of the pocket of his white lab coat. "This is what I meant to give you. It's addressed to all of you," he said.

"Oooh, just feel the quality of this paper," said Blossom, taking the thick, cream-coloured envelope.

"Who cares about the paper – what does it say?" grumbled Buttercup, snatching the envelope out of Blossom's hands and tearing it open. "The Mayor cordially invites you to the Annual Townsville Best Citizen of the Year Award ceremony," she read aloud. "Recognising the good deeds of Townsville's residents … blah, blah, blah," she said, tossing the letter aside.

"Wait!" cried Blossom. "Who's been nominated?" She grabbed the letter and

scanned the list of nominees. "The Mayor's been nominated," she said.

"That's totally fair," said Buttercup sarcastically.

"And Dr Dee Kay," read Blossom. "For services to dentistry and oral hygiene."

"Get flossed," said Buttercup.

"Candy Honeydew has been nominated too," said Blossom. "She's a primary school teacher who spends her weekends picking up litter and volunteering for the Hats for Homeless Squirrels charity."

"Aw," said Bubbles. "That sounds like a really good cause. Squirrels are so cute!"

"Why do squirrels need hats?" grumbled Buttercup. "Don't they have fur on their heads already?"

"There's one more nominee," said Blossom. "It's—" She blinked twice and passed the letter to Bubbles. "I'm so tired my eyes are playing tricks on me."

Bubbles read the letter and gasped. "Princess Morbucks?!"

"I guess my eyes are OK after all," said Blossom.

Bubbles continued to read the letter out loud. "Princess Morbucks has been nominated for her extremely generous donations to the Princess Morbucks Community Centre, the Princess Morbucks Playground, the Princess Morbucks Library, the Princess Morbucks Bike Rack and the Princess Morbucks Drinking Fountain."

"The only reason she's been nominated is because she's rich," said Blossom, disgusted.

"She just buys everything she wants."

"Not everything," said Buttercup. "She can't buy superpowers."

"Not that she hasn't tried," said Bubbles.

"Yeah, you can't buy your way into The Powerpuff Girls," Buttercup said, remembering all the times Princess Morbucks had tried – and failed – to become a superhero. She chuckled. "We're priceless!"

"Ugh – listen to this," said Bubbles, wrinkling her nose and reading in a singsong voice like Princess Morbucks. "'I'm DEEPLY humbled by this nomination. It's SUCH an honour to be included alongside my fellow nominees.'"

"Pass the sick bag," said Buttercup, pretending to throw up.

"I feel sooooooooo fortunate!" sang Bubbles, fluffing her hair in a perfect imitation of Princess Morbucks. "Because I've got a FORTUNE!"

Buttercup laughed so hard that tears rolled down her cheeks. "Stop, Bubbs!" she

gasped, clutching her sides. "I'm gonna pee!"

But Blossom wasn't laughing. She wasn't even smiling.

"What's wrong, Blossom?" Bubbles asked her. "Was my imitation too mean?"

Blossom shook her head. "It's not that," she said sadly.

"Are you upset because Princess Morbucks has been nominated?" asked Buttercup.

"No," said Blossom. "I'm upset because of who *hasn't* been nominated."

"Sorry, I'm still not getting it," said Buttercup.

Think! Who does LOTS and LOTS for Townsville and never asks for anything in return …

Buttercup and Bubbles stared at their sister blankly.

"Us!" said Blossom. "The Powerpuff Girls! We're not on the list!"

Realisation finally dawned on Buttercup and Bubbles. The nominations for Townsville Best Citizen of the Year were TOTALLY UNFAIR!

POWERPUFFS ON PARADE

"Hang on a minute – are you telling me that somebody thinks that Princess Morbucks is a better citizen than us?" Buttercup asked incredulously.

"Not just Princess Morbucks," said Bubbles, glancing down at the invitation.

"The Mayor, Dr Dee Kay and Candy Honeydew too."

"That's ridiculous," said Buttercup. "None of them would even be here any more if it wasn't for us!"

"That's right," said Blossom, nodding. "After all, who did the Mayor call when that exploding volcano almost wiped out Townsville?"

"Us!" cried Bubbles.

"Everyone in town would have been washed away if we hadn't held back the wave," said Blossom.

"Not Princess Morbucks," said Buttercup. "She would have floated past, waving from her luxury super yacht."

"That's the only super thing about her!" said Bubbles.

"Nice one, Bubbs," chuckled Buttercup, giving her sister a high five.

Blossom thought of all the other times The Powerpuff Girls had saved Townsville from ruin. The hotline from the Mayor's office to their bedroom hardly ever stopped ringing!

"Townsville would have been destroyed if we hadn't tamed that yeti," Blossom reminded her sisters, her indignation mounting.

"Yeah, Dr Tooth Dee Kay wouldn't even have an office left if it wasn't for us," said Buttercup.

The Powerpuff Girls paced up and down the living room, growing angrier and angrier.

"There should only be three names on

the shortlist," said
Blossom.

"Yeah!" yelled
Buttercup. "Blossom, Bubbles
and Buttercup!"

"Maybe Candy Honeydew, too,"
said Bubbles. "Because squirrels do
lose a lot of heat from their heads …"

"You're wearing tracks in the carpet,
girls," said Professor Utonium. "If you need
me, I'll be in my lab. I'm working on
technology to reverse the effects of
radiation."

The Powerpuff Girls barely heard him.
They were still furious about the
nominations.

"We don't fight crime for the recognition,"
fumed Blossom. "But it would be nice to feel

a teeny, tiny bit appreciated."

"We've saved Townsville so many times that everyone takes us for granted," said Buttercup.

A plan started to form in Blossom's head. "Maybe we should go on strike," she said. "No monster fighting for a week!"

"It seems a shame to let our superpowers go to waste," said Bubbles.

"Yeah," said Buttercup. "I don't want to stop beating up baddies."

"Then we'll just have to go somewhere else," said Blossom. "Someplace where we won't be taken for granted."

But where — oh where — could that be?

Blossom, Bubbles and Buttercup went upstairs to their bedroom to do some

research. Blossom sat down at the computer and logged in. An advertisement popped up on the screen. *Visit Villageton!* read the ad. It had a picture of a pretty town square and there was a telephone number to call for more information.

"Maybe we should go to the forest," said Bubbles dreamily. "There are loads of amazing animals there ..."

"Can you get pizza there?" asked Buttercup. "If not, count me out."

"I was thinking somewhere closer to home," Blossom said. "Maybe we should check out Villageton – it looks nice."

She rang the telephone number on the screen.

"Hello," said Blossom. "Could you please tell me more about Villageton?"

There was a long pause as she listened to the person on the other end of the line. "Oooh," she said. "Oh dear. It sounds as if you could use some help. See you soon."

She hung up the phone and smiled at her sisters.

"Well?" asked Buttercup.

"That was the Mayoress. Villageton was attacked by a volcano monster last week and there was a toxic waste spill the week before," said Blossom.

"They really need us," said Bubbles happily. "It sounds perfect!"

"What are we waiting for?" said Buttercup. "Let's go!"

The Powerpuff Girls zoomed off in a blaze of light.

"So long, suckers!" cried Buttercup as

they flew over Townsville and crossed the border into Villageton.

> *There's a saying that the grass is always greener on the other side. In Villageton the grass WAS greener — thanks to the toxic waste spill that had left everything fluorescent green!*

As they flew into the centre of Villageton, The Powerpuff Girls spotted an old man struggling with a heavy bag of shopping.

"Let me help you with that," said Buttercup. She scooped up the shopping bag – and the old man – and flew them home. She was back in a flash, dusting her hands. "That old dude was totally awesome," she said, showing the other a handful of boiled sweets. "He gave use these."

The girls flew on, sucking the boiled sweets. "Wait!" Bubbles cried, as they went past a tree. "Do you hear that?"

Meow! The pitiful sound was coming from a kitten stuck up a tree.

"Hang on, little kitty!" called Bubbles. She

flew up to the branch and gently carried the kitten to safety.

The girls set off again but before they'd gone far Blossom noticed a lady washing windows. She was standing on a ladder, stretching to reach the top of the window with her squeegee. Suddenly, she lost her footing and started to fall!

"Oh no!" Blossom gasped. She swooped down and caught the lady just before she hit the ground. Then Blossom quickly finished washing the lady's windows.

"There!" said Blossom, handing the lady her squeegee. "Squeaky clean!"

Eventually, the Powerpuff Girls approached the centre of Villageton.

"Looks like there's some kind of celebration going on," said Blossom.

In the town square, a marching band played and cheerleaders twirled batons. There was a float decorated with flowers with three thrones on it. As The Powerpuff Girls landed, everyone applauded.

"They're here!" cried the crowd.

"Three cheers for The Powerpuff Girls!" said a woman wearing a sash with medals pinned to it.

"HIP HIP HOORAY!" shouted the crowd.

"Wow!" said Blossom, her eyes shining. "Is all of this for us?"

"Of course," said the woman with the sash. "The second you called our hotline I started arranging it. It is such an honour to have you here. I'm the Mayoress of Villageton. I welcome you to our humble town." The Mayoress presented each of the girls with a medal. "There," she said, pinning them on. "Now you are all VIP citizens of Villageton."

Leading Blossom, Bubbles and Buttercup over to the float, the Mayoress climbed up

and pointed to three thrones in the middle. "Take a seat so your welcome parade can get started," she told them.

The Powerpuff Girls exchanged excited looks as they perched on the thrones. A marching band launched into *For She's a Jolly Good Fellow* as the parade set off through the streets of Villageton. Blossom, Bubbles and Buttercup waved to the crowd as cheerleaders shook their pom-poms and tossed their batons high in the air.

"Now this is more like it!" said Blossom, soaking up the applause.

"I could definitely get used to this," said Bubbles, sighing happily.

People lining the streets threw handfuls of tiny, colourful objects on to the float.

"Is that confetti?" asked Blossom.

But it wasn't confetti. It was—

"Candy!!!!!!!" squealed Bubbles, as they were showered with sweets.

"Outta my way!" shouted Buttercup, scrabbling around to scoop up as much candy as she could hold.

"Grthmurph!" said Blossom through a mouthful of candy.

I think what Blossom's trying to say is: "This is amazing!"

"Woo hoo!" shouted Buttercup, cramming candy into her mouth. "I love this place!"

As The Powerpuff Girls munched their way to an epic sugar high, the Mayoress of Villageton held a meeting in her office.

"Stage One is complete," said the Mayoress.

"My plan is working even better than I'd hoped," gloated a red-haired girl in a tiara.

"You can count on me to deliver Stage Two," said the Mayoress. "But I will require further payment."

"One million, two million, three million," said the girl, counting out a huge wad of banknotes and tossing them

one by one on to the Mayoress's desk.

"It's a pleasure doing business with you, Princess Moreucks," the Mayoress, quickly gathering up the money.

"Keep the change," said Princess Morbucks, grinning.

Oh no! Princess Morbucks has something terrible up her sleeve (and not just a snotty tissue, like me)! I hate to rain on The Powerpuff Girls' parade, but this does NOT look good.

SPOTLIGHT ON
THE POWERPUFF GIRLS

> *That night, The Powerpuff Girls dreamed about pom-poms, parades and sweets of all kinds. Princess Morbucks also had sweet dreams – about pummelling The Powerpuff Girls!*

"Rise and shine, girls!" Professor Utonium called up the stairs. "Breakfast is ready!"

"Ugh," groaned Buttercup, rolling over in bed. "I'm still stuffed from all that candy we ate yesterday."

"Maybe we'll get some more today!" said Bubbles, bouncing up and down as she hugged Octi. She was still feeling hyper.

Blossom hopped out of bed. "I'm going to brush my teeth. I flossed twice last night but I can still taste sugar."

Downstairs, the Professor served up a scientifically balanced breakfast of scrambled eggs, wholegrain toast and orange juice.

"Any plans for today?" asked the Professor, picking up the newspaper. He scanned the headlines. "It says here that a bull is on the loose in Townsville, so I'm sure you'll be getting a call from the Mayor."

"We won't be here to help him," said Blossom, buttering her toast.

"We'll be in Villageton, where our superpowers are appreciated," said Bubbles.

"And people give us candy," said Buttercup, pushing eggs around her plate.

"Girls, what have I told you about taking candy from strangers?" said Professor Utonium sternly. "It's NOT a good idea."

You should listen to the Professor, readers!

When they had finished breakfast, The Powerpuff Girls heard the hotline in their bedroom ring. The phone rang and rang but they ignored it.

"I hope the Mayor's wearing a red cape today," said Buttercup. "Since he's going to have to fight that bull on his own."

"I'm sure he'll find some other Best Citizen to help him," sniffed Blossom. "Now let's get out of here."

The Powerpuff Girls headed to the much, much greener pastures of Villageton. As they soared over their adopted town, they waved cheerfully to the people below.

"We love you, Blossom!" called a lady pushing a buggy.

"You sure look cute today, Bubbles!" shouted a little girl walking her dog.

"Way to go, Buttercup!" cheered a boy on a skateboard.

"People are so nice here," said Bubbles.

Maybe a little too nice?

The Powerpuff Girls arrived at the town hall and went straight to the Mayoress's

office. She was counting a huge wad of cash and quickly shoved it in her desk when she saw them.

"Why hello, honorary citizens of Villageton," the Mayoress said, standing up.

"Morning, Mayoress," said Buttercup. "Got any baddies for us to fight?"

"Er, not at the moment," said the Mayoress. "But come and see something that Prin—" She quickly corrected herself. "That I had built especially for you girls."

The thing she wanted to show them was draped in a sheet.

"Ta da!" cried the Mayoress, sweeping off the sheet to unveil a huge spotlight with *PPG* on the lens. "When I need your help, I'll turn the light on and you'll see the letters shining in the sky," she explained. "Do you like it?"

"No," said Bubbles, staring at the light. "I LOVE it!"

"It's awesome," said Buttercup.

"Way better than a stupid hotline," Blossom said, trying to ignore the niggle of concern she felt about Townsville's tiny Mayor fighting a huge bull.

"There's no danger here at the moment," said the Mayoress. "None whatsoever. Not even one teeny tiny itty bit of peril. So why don't you three go and explore your new town."

The Powerpuff Girls shot into the air. They flew over a park, a shopping centre and a school.

"Everything's kind of green," said Bubbles, gazing down.

"Green's my favourite colour," said Buttercup.

"And people in Townsville will be green with envy when they find out we're citizens of Villageton now," said Blossom, laughing.

"Look!" gasped Buttercup.

"A bird!" said Bubbles. "Hello, Mr Robin."

The robin twittered back at her and

Bubbles giggled. "You're so funny," she said, laughing at the bird's joke. Bubbles was the only Powerpuff Girl who had the ability to understand animals.

"Not the bird!" said Buttercup, pointing up into the clouds. "Look at THAT!"

The letters *PPG* were shining high in the sky.

"The Mayoress needs us!" exclaimed Blossom.

"Time to kick some butt!" said Buttercup, punching her palm.

The Powerpuff Girls flew back to the town hall and in through the window, landing in the Mayoress's office. The spotlight was still shining.

"Um, we're here now," said Buttercup, blinking in the bright light. "So you can turn

that thing off."

But instead of switching the spotlight off, the Mayoress swivelled it round so that its dazzling beam shone right in Buttercup's face! The light started to turn green.

"Hey, what gives?" said Buttercup, shielding her eyes.

Next, the Mayoress pointed the spotlight at Bubbles. The light turned blue.

"Ouchie!" cried Bubbles, squinting.

"That's hurting my eyes!"

Then the Mayoress turned the spotlight on Blossom.

"Argh! Too bright!" Blossom cried as the light turned pink.

At last, the Mayoress switched off the light.

"Thank goodness," said Blossom, rubbing her eyes. Her relief was short-lived. The light came on again. This time, it lit up red, curly hair and a gleaming gold tiara. Princess Morbucks basked in the light, grinning smugly as the beam turned pink, then blue, and finally green as it streamed on to her.

Laughing gleefully, Princess Morbucks rose into the air. "I can fly!" she sang out, turning a loop-the-loop and leaving a pink, blue and green-striped trail of light behind

her. "I can FLY!!!!!!!"

"After her!" called Blossom. But when she tried to jump into the air, she landed back down on the ground.

"Hey!" cried Buttercup. "I CAN'T fly!"

"Me neither!" wailed Bubbles. "What's going on?"

"I'll tell you what's going on," gloated Princess Morbucks, hovering in front of them. "The spotlight is my new power ray. It stole your powers and gave them to ME!" Zooming off, she sang out, "Catch you later, gal pals!"

The Powerpuff Girls stared in disbelief until Princess Morbucks was just a tiny dot on the horizon.

"Maybe this isn't as bad as it seems," said Bubbles hopefully.

Buttercup tried to lift the heavy spotlight but she couldn't. "Ugh!" she grunted, straining hard. "I don't have my superstrength any more!"

Blossom squinted her eyes but no red beams came out. "My laser vision is gone!"

"Tell me this is all just a bad dream," Bubbles said to a mouse peeping out of a

hole. The mouse squeaked and ran off. Looking at her sisters in dismay, Bubbles wailed, "I didn't understand a word!"

Blossom nodded sadly. "We've lost our powers. So now we're just … Puff Girls."

Doesn't have quite the same ring, does it?

THE WALK
OF SHAME

> *Robbed of their powers by Princess Morbucks, The*
> *Powerpuff Girls – sorry, I mean The Puff Girls –*
> *decided to go home.*

Without their flying powers, Blossom,
Bubbles and Buttercup started the long walk

back to Townsville. As they trudged through Villageton, the town looked even greener than it had from the air. They passed green trees, green houses and green pavements.

"You know, I'm getting kinda sick of green," said Buttercup, pulling a face.

"Are we there yet?" whined Bubbles.

"No," said Blossom, checking her map. "We have 5.8 more miles to go. And if we continue walking at 3.1 miles per hour, according to my calculations we'll get back home in … 112 minutes."

Good to see that Blossom hasn't lost her mental maths skills!

Bubbles groaned. "I'm getting a blister!" She looked up enviously at a bird flying overhead and shouted, "Do you know how

lucky you are?" The bird squawked in reply. Bubbles sighed. "I have no idea what he said."

"Man, walking is so … ordinary," grumbled Buttercup.

Blossom and Bubbles nodded glumly and they all plodded on.

112 minutes later they reached the centre of Townsville.

A big crowd was gathered outside of the town hall, gazing up at the sky.

"Look, there's Maylyn," said Blossom, pointing to a cool-looking girl wearing roller skates and a helmet. She was the captain of the Derbytantes, Buttercup's deathball team.

> *What do you mean you've never heard of deathball? It's just like roller derby — only about 101% more violent!*

"What's she doing here?" wondered

Buttercup.

There were lots of familiar faces in the crowd – neighbours, kids from school and other townspeople The Powerpuff Girls had helped.

"Hey, Blossom – isn't that Jared Shapiro?" Bubbles asked. She pointed to a dark-haired boy with glasses from their class at school.

"Stop pointing!" Blossom hissed, her cheeks flushing pink. She quickly straightened her hair bow.

PSSSSTTTT! Blossom might just have a teeny tiny crush on Jared.

Just then, Jared spotted the girls hobbling towards the town hall. "They're back!" he cried. "Tell the Mayor – The Powerpuff Girls are back!"

"Yay!" cheered the crowd.

"Hey Blossom!" said Jared.

Blossom blushed as red as her hair bow.

Bubbles' BFF, Donny the Unicorn, rushed over to greet her, using his unicorn magic to make a flag with 'Welcome back!' on it.

"Such a waste of unicorn magic," Buttercup muttered.

"Hi, Donny," said Bubbles, trying not to be jealous that her unicorn best friend still had powers.

"You're looking super-cute today, Bubbles!" Donny said.

"Thanks, Donny," said Bubbles with a sigh. At least she hadn't lost her super-cuteness.

"Girls!" cried the Mayor, peering at them through his monocle. "Thank goodness you returned! I gathered everyone here to welcome you back."

"You probably just want us to deal with the bull that's on the loose," said Buttercup wearily.

"No, it's fine," said the Mayor. "I challenged the bull to a pickle fight, and it turns out he just loves pickles! He's cooking a pickle omelette for me in the café now."

"Glad to hear you're managing without our superpowers," said Blossom. "Because that's how it's going to be from now on."

"I'm so sorry to have upset you, girls," said the Mayor. "There's been a big misunderstanding."

"What?" said Buttercup indignantly. "You

mean you DON'T think that Dr Dee Kay is a better citizen than us?"

"Of course not," said the Mayor. "Dr Dee Kay doesn't even exist. The awards ceremony was just a clever ruse to throw you a We Love The Powerpuff Girls surprise party!"

"Oh! That's so sweet!" said Bubbles.

"Whose idea was that?" asked Blossom, pretty sure she knew the answer already.

"Princess Morbucks suggested it," said the Mayor. "She said she had a brilliant plan."

"Her plan *was* brilliant," said Blossom. "Literally. She stole all our powers with a brilliant light!"

"Oh dear," said the Mayor, wringing his hands. "I'm such a fool! I never should have listened to Princess Morbucks. But she can be very persuasive – she even offered to pay for the party and hold it in the Princess Morbucks Recreation Centre."

"Well, you can cancel the party," said Buttercup. "There's nothing to celebrate any more."

"You can disconnect the hotline, too," said Bubbles, dejected. "We're no use to Townsville."

"Or anywhere else," said Blossom, a tear rolling down her cheek.

"Don't be silly," said the Mayor. "You three are still Townsville's best citizens – with or without your superpowers."

"That's right," said Jared Shapiro. "We

love you." Blushing, he quickly clarified, "I meant the plural form of you, not the singular."

"You're all, like, totally amazing!" said Donny the Unicorn, swishing his yellow tail.

"Are you going to take this lying down?" Maylyn asked Buttercup.

"I'm not lying down," grumbled Buttercup. "But I wish I was – my feet are killing me!"

"That's not what I meant," said Maylyn, her hands on her hips. "Are you going to let Princess Morbucks get away with this?"

"What are we supposed to do?" Blossom protested. "Princess Morbucks took all our powers."

"I say we kick Princess Morbucks's butt!" cried Maylyn.

"Yeah!" the Derbytantes replied.

Everyone joined in as the Derbytantes' started chanting, "KICK HER BUTT!"

"Do you really mean it?" asked Blossom.

"You three have helped us so many times," said the Mayor. "Now it's time for the citizens of Townsville to help you."

"I'll ask the Unicorn Coalition Alliance Brigade to help," said Donny.

"Let's go and kick some princess butt!" roared Maylyn.

TIME TO KICK BUTT!

> The citizens of Townsville showered The Powerpuff Girls with love. It wasn't as tasty as being showered with candy, but it was better for their teeth!

"They're right," said Buttercup. "We don't need our superpowers to kick butt."

"Princess Morbucks might have taken our powers, but she hasn't stolen the most important thing of all," said Blossom.

"Our cuteness?" guessed Bubbles.

"No!" said Blossom. "Our fighting spirit!"

"True dat!" cried Donny.

"Bring me a flip chart!" cried Blossom.

The Mayor dashed into the town hall and came back carrying a flip chart taller than he was.

"We still have lots of skills that aren't superpowers," said Blossom. "I'm good at planning, so I'll be in charge of organisation."

"Can I help?" asked Jared Shapiro eagerly.

"Of course," said Blossom, her cheeks turning pink again.

"I'll head up military operations," said

Buttercup. "I can train the troops."

"Perfect," said Blossom, scribbling on the flip chart.

"Attention!" called Buttercup. The Derbytantes and a motorcycle gang with leather jackets and huge beards formed a double line and saluted Buttercup. "Forward march!" commanded Buttercup.

"What should I do?" asked Bubbles.

"You can lead the animal army," said Blossom.

"But I can't understand them any more," said Bubbles, stroking a stray dog sadly.

"That doesn't matter," said Blossom as the dog nuzzled Bubbles. "They still love you anyway. You might not be able to talk to them, but they still understand you!"

"I'm sure my squirrels will be happy to

help," said a sweet-looking lady wearing a hand-knitted cardigan and matching bobble hat. "I'm Candy Honeydew."

"Oh!" said Mayor, surprised. "I thought I'd made you up!"

Soon nearly everyone in Townsville was busy with the war effort. Blossom and Jared hurried to the library and pored over maps of Villageton.

Blossom pointed to a hill. "We should launch our attack from high ground."

"Look!" said Jared, studying a blueprint of the town hall. "There's a secret underground entrance."

In the park, Buttercup blew a whistle and her troops jogged and rollerskated over to her.

"Hit the ground and give me 100 push-

ups!" Buttercup bellowed.

Bubbles had recruited a platoon of Townsville's pets. There were dogs, cats, birds, bunnies, two pet snakes and even an enormous chinchillasaurus.

Bubbles held up a picture of Princess Morbucks's freckled face and pointed at it. "When you see this princess, ATTACK!" she commanded.

"Grrrr!" growled the animals, baring

their teeth (if they had them).

As Blossom and Jared left the library, they bumped into Professor Utonium returning a huge stack of library books. "What's going on?" he asked.

"Princess Morbucks stole our powers with a power ray," explained Blossom. "So we're raising an army to stop her."

"Can I help?" the Professor asked.

Blossom suddenly had an amazing idea. "Do you have any Chemical X left? she asked hopefully.

> *Flashback – Chemical X was what Professor Utonium accidentally added when he was creating The Powerpuff Girls. It gave them their superpowers!*

"Unfortunately not," said the Professor. "I used up my whole supply and I can't get any more."

Blossom's face fell. She had been hoping that if she and her sisters drank some Chemical X they might get their powers back.

"But the reverse radiation technology I've been developing might be useful," said Professor Utonium. "I might be able to reverse the power ray."

"That would be awesome!" exclaimed Blossom. She hurried to tell her sisters the plan.

Back in the town square, things were going well.

"You've passed Buttercup's Boot Camp," Buttercup told her soldiers. "You're ready to go to war!"

The animal army was looking good, too. The Unicorn Coalition Alliance Brigade had flown in and were stamping their hooves, ready for battle. A squadron of squirrels, all wearing woolly hats, practised throwing acorns at a target with the picture of Princess Morbucks stuck to it.

"Bullseye!" cried Bubbles.

"Listen up," shouted Blossom. "We're going to march into Villageton and attack from high ground. Then we'll capture the town hall so the Professor can reverse the power ray."

"Who wants some face paint?" asked Donny the Unicorn holding up a hoof-ful of paint.

Blossom painted on fierce stripes of pink paint.

Buttercup daubed scary green zigzags on her forehead.

Bubbles painted blue hearts on her cheeks.

"Dude, it's meant to be WARPAINT!" said Buttercup.

"Haven't you ever heard that love conquers all?" said Bubbles sweetly.

Led by their commanders Blossom, Bubbles and Buttercup, the Townsville troops marched into Villageton. This time, nobody cheered or waved.

"Watch out!" whimpered a man, ducking behind a tree.

"Take cover!" shouted a lady, diving under a bush.

"Weird," said Blossom. "Last time they were so welcoming."

"It must be because we're so scary-looking," said Bubbles, holding a fluffy white kitten in her arms.

Yeah, that's proabably it …

Suddenly, the ground trembled.

Professor Utonium frowned. "That's strange," he said. "My seismograph back at the lab didn't detect any earthquakes."

The ground shook again. This time, buildings wobbled, branches fell off trees and roof tiles smashed on the ground.

The Townsville army marched around a corner and let out a collective gasp.

"Uh oh," said Blossom.

Princess Morbucks was zooming around the town centre, crashing into buildings and knocking down signposts. Her entourage, the Cash Money Krew, egged her on from the ground, wearing gold-plated hard hats.

"Wheeeee!" Princess Morbucks cried, diving to the ground then bashing into a bus stop.

"Learn how to fly!" Buttercup shouted at her as she zoomed past.

Pink light shimmered in the air then took the shape of a tape dispenser.

"That's MY aura power!" cried Blossom, horrified as the tape dispenser wound sticky tape round and round a frightened man waiting at the bus stop.

The pink light turned green and transformed into a bulldozer.

"Now it's my aura!" said Buttercup. She watched, outraged, as her bulldozer aura ploughed into a parked car, flipping it over.

"Hey! Cut it out!" Buttercup yelled.

Then the light turned blue and became a T-Rex. The T-Rex roared, then lumbered around, toppling buildings.

"What's she doing with Rexy?" wailed Bubbles. It was bad enough that Princess Morbucks was using her animal aura – but she was doing it so badly!

"It's worse than we thought," Blossom said grimly. "She's completely out of control!"

Quick, Blossom! It's time for a new plan!

SHOW ME THE MONEY

> *Princess Morbucks was terrorising Villageton with The Powerpuff Girls' auras!*

"Let's take her down," Blossom said.

"CHARGE!" ordered Buttercup.

The deathball players and hairy bikers flung themselves at Princess Morbucks, punching and kicking. Even though they were all twice her size, they were no match for her superstrength and superspeed. Their blows glanced off her harmlessly, barely ruffling her curly red hair.

Laughing, Princess Morbucks swatted away one of the Derbytantes. "You'll need to try harder than that, gal pal!"

"Bubbles," said Blossom. "Send in the animal army."

"ATTACK!" cried Bubbles. Growling and yowling, dogs and cats pounced on Princess Morbucks.

"Bad doggies! Bad kitties!" Princess Morbucks said. Whimpering, the pet platoon retreated, tails between their legs.

The unicorns charged at Princess Morbucks, their heads lowered.

"Olé!" she cried gleefully, zooming into the air to avoid their horns.

From the ground, squirrels in woolly hats pelted her with acorns and conkers.

PING! PING! PING!

"Nice hats," jeered Princess Morbucks,

uninjured. "Where can I buy one? Rodents-R-Us?"

Her T-Rex aura roared and chased the Townsville animal army away.

Nothing was working!

"We need reinforcements," said Blossom.

"I'll help you!" volunteered a man from Villageton.

"Me too!" said an old lady.

The citizens of Villageton stepped forward. "We hate what Princess Morbucks is doing to our town," said a teenaged girl.

Side by side, the citizens of Villageton and Townsville battled valiantly. But even the combined forces couldn't stop the fabulously rich, flame-haired menace. She swooped around recklessly, leaving a trail of destruction in her wake. They needed a

NEW new plan!

Blossom, Bubbles and Buttercup huddled together under a picnic table.

"We need to get the Professor into the town hall," said Blossom.

"But how?" asked Buttercup. "Our military might is no match for her – I mean OUR – superpowers."

"What does Princess Morbucks like more than anything else in the world?" said Blossom.

"That's easy," said Bubbles. "Money!"

KACHIIIIIIING!

"Exactly!" said Blossom, an idea beginning to form in her mind.

"Let's create a distraction, then infiltrate the town hall …"

> LOOK OUT! THERE'S A HUGE, HAIRY TARANTULA RIGHT BEHIND YOU
> *(See, distraction can be a very effective tactic!)*

"Yoo hoo! Princess Morbucks," shouted Donny the Unicorn. "Someone broke into the Villageton Savings Bank. They're stealing all the money from your safe!"

"NOOOOOOO!" cried Princess Morbucks. She flew straight to the bank. "Show me the money!" she demanded.

The manager led her into the bank vault – then locked her in!

"Yay!" cheered the people of Townsville and Villageton.

But Princess Morbucks was too strong to

be trapped for long. There was no time to lose!

Professor Utonium and The Powerpuff Girls ran to the town hall as fast as they could.

"I – can't – breathe," huffed Blossom.

"I've got a stitch," puffed Bubbles, clutching her side.

"You two really need to get more exercise," said Buttercup.

"No, we just need to get our powers back," said Blossom.

The Mayoress was guarding the town hall's entrance with Princess Morbucks's pet white tiger.

"Madam," said Professor Utonium. "Would you please let us in so that I could make a small, er, repair."

"Sorry," said the Mayoress, blocking their way. "No can do. Villageton has been strapped for cash since that unfortunate toxic waste spill. Princess Morbucks paid me a fortune."

"Did you hear that?" Blossom asked her sisters. "That was the sound of all my illusions shattering." She shook her head sadly. "Maybe I won't go into politics after all …"

"Figure out your career later, Bloss," cried Buttercup. "Let's go!"

They ran to the back of the town hall, where Jared had located a secret entrance on the blueprint. Unfortunately, the 'secret entrance'

was actually an old sewage pipe.

"Pee yew!" said Bubbles, ducking into the slimy tunnel. "This stinks."

"Gross!" said Blossom.

"Did you know that human beings can detect one trillion different smells?" Professor Utonium informed them as they crawled through the sewage system.

"Well this is one I could definitely do without," Buttercup said, holding her nose.

Eventually, they climbed out of the tunnel into a dingy basement.

"We're in the *bowels* of the town hall," said Blossom.

"Phew! I'm *pooped*," said Bubbles.

"Way to go, Bloss," said Buttercup. "That plan didn't totally *stink*!"

"We need to get to the Mayoress's office,"

said Blossom, heading upstairs.

As they went, Professor Utonium pulled out a calculator. "Er, girls," he said. "I don't mean to worry you, but there's something you should know."

"If it's that girls have a better sense of smell than boys, I know that," said Blossom.

Genuine scientific fact alert!

"No," said the Professor, shaking his head. "I've been doing some calculations and if I can't reverse the ray in the next hour it won't work at all."

"You mean ... " said Bubbles.

"We'll lose our powers for ever!" shrieked Blossom.

PROFESSOR UTONIUM TO THE RESCUE

The clock was ticking! If Professor Utonium could't reverse the power ray then The Powerpuff Girls would stay ordinary for ever. Can you imagine?

They ran up two flight of stairs.

"I think the Mayoress's office is this way!" panted Bubbles.

They burst through a door and found a

cleaner sitting on the toilet reading a copy of
Roller Derby Enthusiast magazine.

Haven't we had enough toilet humour in this book?

"Hey!" he said, annoyed. "Try knocking."

"Oops!" said Bubbles. "Wrong door."

"Can I borrow that when you're done?"
said Buttercup, who still hadn't had a chance
to read that month's issue.

"Focus, Buttercup!" said Blossom. "We
don't have time to catch up on our reading."

Behind the next door was a stationery
supply cupboard stuffed full of pens, pencils
and paper emblazoned with the Villageton
crest.

"Oooooh," said Blossom, her eyes wide.

"Focus, Blossom!" mimicked Buttercup,
pulling her sister away from the tempting

selection of stationery.

"Bingo!" said Bubbles, opening the third door.

"We don't have time for games, either," said Blossom, exasperated.

"No, I meant this is the right room," said Bubbles.

The Mayoress's office looked very different to the last time they had been in there. There was a glitzy chandelier, a fancy coffee machine, and a full-length portrait of Princess Morbucks hanging on the wall. A sleek new computer rested on a gold desk next to a 3D printer and a state-of-the-art sound system.

Buttercup whistled. "Looks like the Mayoress went on a spending spree."

The power ray was shoved in a corner, covered by a sheet so that it didn't clash with the new decor. Blossom whipped off the sheet.

"That's a fine piece of machinery," said the Professor, gazing at the power ray admiringly. "I almost wish I'd invented it myself."

"Stop geeking out, Professor," Buttercup

told him. "And start reversing it!"

Professor Utonium opened up his briefcase, revealing an array of scientific instruments. Taking out a complicated-looking tool, he quickly took the power ray apart and studied the parts.

"Right," he said, clapping his hands together. "First I'll need to neutralise the electron field to reverse the magnetic charge."

"Ooh! Can I help?" Blossom asked eagerly.

"Of course," said Professor Utonium. "Why don't you isolate the diffraction matrix and condense the spectrum while I split the atoms?"

That sounds like totally real, not even slightly made-up science. Right?

While the Professor and Blossom were busy working on the power ray, Bubbles and Buttercup explored the Mayoress's office.

"If it was my office, I'd hang up some pictures of cute puppies and kittens," said Bubbles.

Bored, Buttercup tossed a diamond-encrusted paperweight up and down. "I wonder if that guy's done with his magazine yet?"

Sitting in the Mayoress's new swivel chair and spinning round and round, Bubbles started singing the *Space Towtruck* theme tune loudly.

"Shush, Bubbles," said Blossom, looking up from the component she was assembling. "Some of us are trying to concentrate!"

Sighing, Bubbles wandered over to the

window and looked out.

"Oh no!" she gasped, catching sight of a pink, blue and green light streaking through the sky. "Princess Morbucks has escaped from the bank!"

"Hurry!" said Buttercup. "You need to fix the ray before she gets here!"

Blossom quickly handed the component to the Professor, who fitted it back inside the power ray.

"There! That should reverse the effects," said Professor Utonium, giving the lens a polish. "Let's fire it up." Professor Utonium flicked the switch but no light shone out of the power ray.

He toggled the switch again.

Nothing happened.

"Hmm," said the Professor. "That's odd."

"Dude!" Buttercup exclaimed. "It's not plugged in."

Sometimes even the cleverest people can be a bit dim.

Buttercup ran over to the power socket, where electrical leads from all of the Mayoress's new gadgets were tangled like a heap of high-tech spaghetti.

Buttercup plugged in a red lead. Country and western music blared out of the sound system, making everyone jump.

"Oops! Not that one," said Buttercup, yanking out the lead.

She tried a blue lead. The 3D printer started whirring and spewing out lots of minature plastic statues of Princess Morbucks.

"Wrong again!" cried Blossom.

"She's nearly here!" Bubbles wailed, glancing out of the window.

Sweat poured down Buttercup's face as she pulled out the blue lead. *Which one is it?* she thought desperately.

Princess Morbucks flew through the office window and landed on the Mayoress's desk. "Nice try, gal pals," she said, straightening her tiara. "But that necronium-steel bank vault was no match for my superstrength."

"You mean OUR superstrength!" said Bubbles.

"Now, Buttercup!" yelled Blossom.

Hoping for the best, Buttercup jammed a yellow lead into the socket.

Let there be light!

Brilliant light streamed out of the power ray. Blossom pointed it at Princess Morbucks and the beam turned pink, then blue and then green.

"Stop that!" screamed Princess Morbucks. Trying to escape from the dazzling light, she jumped off the Mayoress's desk. Instead of flying into the air, she landed on her bottom.

"Hey!" she shrieked. "Where have my superpowers gone?"

Professor Utonium patted the power ray. "They've been reversed, thanks to my soon-to-be-patented technology."

"AAARRGGGH!" Princess Morbucks's face went the same shade of red as her hair. Furious, she charged at them. Professor

Utonium and The Powerpuff Girls formed a wall to protect the power ray. Even though she'd lost her superstrength, Princess Morbucks still fought like a tiger.

Her extremely rare, incredibly expensive pet white tiger, to be precise.

"Oh no, you don't," said the Mayoress, running into her office. She whipped off her mayor's sash and tied Princess Morbucks up with it.

"This was NOT the deal!" Princess Morbucks.

"The deal's off," said the Mayoress miserably. "I thought that money and fancy gadgets were more important than the welfare of my citizens. Now I see how wrong I was."

"Wow. Maybe I WILL run for president after all," Blossom said.

Yay! Blossom's belief in the political system has been restored!

"Fine," said Buttercup impatiently. "But there's a little something we need to do first …"

Professor Utonium turned the power ray's beam towards Blossom. Pink light streamed out, giving Blossom a rosy glow.

Then he pointed the beam at Bubbles, bathing her in beautiful blue light.

Finally, the Professor directed the power ray at Buttercup, hitting her with a dazzling beam of green light.

The Powerpuff Girls held their breath. Had it worked?

Holding hands, Blossom, Bubbles and Buttercup jumped into the air – and flew!

For the second time in their lives, Professor Utonium had given Blossom, Bubbles and Buttercup superpowers!

PARTY POWER!

> *Hooray! The Powerpuff Girls can fly again. But have they got ALL of their superpowers back?*

In the tussle with Princess Morbucks, the Mayoress's desk had been knocked over and the bin had fallen on its side, spilling out bits of paper. If there was one thing Blossom hated more than crime, injustice and political corruption, it was mess!

"Time for the moment of truth," said Blossom. She summoned up a glowing pink light. It turned into a broom. Her aura was back!

SWEEP! SWEEP! SWEEP!

Blossom's broom aura tidied up the office.

"Phew!" she said, relieved. "Cleaning is so much quicker when you've got superpowers."

"Let me give you a hand," said Buttercup. She picked up the desk with one hand and set it back down, the right way up. "I've got my superstrength back!" she said, flexing her biceps.

Shrieks of terror came from outside. Princess Morbucks's white tiger was still guarding the town hall, pacing up and down and growling at passers-by.

"I'll deal with this!" Bubbles said, flying out of the window.

"Bad kitty!" Bubbles told the tiger sternly. "Go home!"

The tiger yawned lazily.

"Shoo!" Bubbles said.

The tiger flicked its tail.

Uh oh, Bubbles thought. *Maybe I've lost my ability to speak to animals for ever.*

She tried one more time. "Go back to Princess Morbucks's mansion!" Bubbles shouted.

The tiger growled at her.

Bubbles gasped. "How DARE you speak to me that way!"

Yay! Bubbles CAN still understand animals.

"OK," said Bubbles. "You asked for it." Shimmering blue light shone out of her and turned into a T-Rex.

ROOOOAAAAARRRR!

Bubbles' T-Rex aura stomped towards the tiger, waving its stubby arms and baring its razor-sharp teeth. Yowling in fright, the tiger fled the T-Rex and bounded away from Villageton.

"Way to go, Rexy!" Bubbles cheered.

Back in the Mayoress's office, the Professor rubbed his eyes. "I think the light from the power ray might have damaged my vision," he said, blinking. "Everything outside looks slightly green."

"No," said the Mayoress, sighing. "That's how Villageton has looked ever since we had that unfortunate (and totally not my fault) toxic waste spill."

"Hmm," said the Professor. "I wonder ..."

He pointed the power ray out of the window. A beam of bright light streamed out, hitting the buildings and streets of Villageton. Professor Utonium turned the dial as high as it could go and the light grew stronger, illuminating the whole town.

Slowly, the bright green began to fade as the power ray reversed the damage.

The toxic tint got fainter and fainter in the powerful light. Soon, the only green things were trees and grass and Brussels sprouts and … bogies!

"My hero!" said the Mayoress, smiling at the Professor.

"I'm just a scientist," Professor Utonium said, blushing modestly. "My girls are the real heroes."

Blossom, Bubbles and Buttercup hugged Professor Utonium.

"You are a hero," said Blossom.

"You're OUR hero," said Bubbles.

"Even if you are kind of a wimpybutt," Buttercup added, grinning.

"Can I give you a ride back to Townsville?" offered the Mayoress.

The Powerpuff Girls shook their heads.

"No thanks," said Blossom. "We'll fly!"

As the Professor climbed into the Mayoress's car, The Powerpuff Girls soared over the no-longer-toxic Villageton landscape.

"I can't wait to get home," said Blossom. "I wonder how old you have to be to run for president?"

"Me neither," said Bubbles. "I'm going to write to my panda pen pal and tell him all about what happened today."

"I'm going to binge-watch *Space Towtruck* series twenty-seven," said Buttercup.

But as they neared Townsville, they could see that a huge crowd had gathered outside the town hall.

"Uh oh," said Blossom, sighing. "We'd better go check if something's wrong."

A superhero's work is NEVER done!

As soon as the The Powerpuff Girls landed, the Mayor hurried over to them, his arms outstretched. "Welcome to the First Annual Powerpuff Girls Street Party!" he exclaimed.

"Say what?" said Buttercup, confused.

"THE FIRST ANNUAL WE LOVE THE POWERPUFF GIRLS STREET PARTY TO CELEBRATE BLOSSOM, BUBBLES AND BUTTERCUP: TOWNSVILLE'S BEST CITIZENS OF THE DECADE!" said

Bubbles, reading a banner that was so long it stretched the full length of Townsville's high street.

Catchy!

"We're so grateful that you came back," said the Mayor. "I'm sorry we haven't always told you how important you three are to us. So I have decreed that there will be a street party every year to celebrate The Powerpuff Girls and all you do for Townsville."

For once the Mayor has actually made a good decision!

"And Villageton, too!" cried the Mayoress, who had just arrived with Professor Utonium.

"Hit it!" the Mayor told a pop band. The blond-haired lead singer started crooning a song they'd written specially.

The Powerpuff Girls rock our town.
They never, never, never ever let us down.
We love Blossom, Bubbles and Buttercup too,
We'd be lost and lonely without you!

"OMG," shrieked Blossom, recognising the sound of their favourite pop band. "It's Sensitive Thugz!"

"I love you, Chance!" Bubbles screamed to the lead singer.

"Woo hoo!" shouted Maylyn and the other Derbytantes. "The Powerpuff Girls rock!"

As Buttercup crowd-surfed with the deathball players, Bubbles and Donny the Unicorn boogied along to the Sensitive Thugz.

"You're the best, Bubbles," said Donny.

"No – YOU are!" squealed Bubbles, hugging her BFF.

"Er, would you care to dance?" Jared Shapiro asked Blossom shyly.

"I'd love to!" Blossom gushed. Then she shrugged and said, "I mean, yeah, OK, sure, why not."

Soon, the whole town was dancing.

The Mayor twirled the Mayoress around.
Even Professor Utonium was doing his
signature dance move, the Electron Charge.

> *To do the Electron Charge, simply point your index finger and shake your whole body vigorously as if you've just been electrocuted. Try it at your next school disco!*

As the Sensitive Thugz launched into a
slow ballad called *UR My Girl, Girl*, The
Powerpuff Girls took a break from dancing.

"I'm starving!" said Buttercup.

The bull was cooking up tasty treats in the
refreshments tent. While Blossom, Bubbles
and Buttercup tucked into a Powerpuff Girls
Surprise – a mound of cream puffs with
strawberry, blueberry and pistachio fillings –
the Mayor came up to them munching a
deep-fried pickle.

"Er, girls," he said. "I really hate to bother you at your own party, but that dragon monster is back …"

Swallowing a cream cake whole, Buttercup stood up. "That monster picked the wrong town to mess with!"

Without a second thought, The Powerpuff Girls flew to the rescue. At the harbour, an enormous dragon monster was flying over the water, setting boats on fire as it passed.

"Put that fire out!" Bubbles demanded.

The dragon monster hissed and used his tail to capsize another ship.

"Wrong decision, buddy boy," said Buttercup, pushing up her sleeves.

As The Powerpuff Girls fought the dragon monster, the sounds of their party echoed in the distance.

"I know we don't do it for the praise, but it's so nice to be appreciated," said Blossom happily. She punched the dragon. **POW!**

"It made me realise something," said Bubbles. "I don't tell you two how much you mean to me often enough. I love you guys." She aimed a karate chop at the dragon. **BLAM!**

"Right back at you, sis," said Buttercup. She kicked the dragon. **WALLOP!**

Then, using all their superhuman strength, The Powerpuff Girls flung the dragon far, far out to sea. **SPLASH!**

"And never come back!" shouted Buttercup, fistbumping her sisters.

Three cheers for The Powerpuff Girls.
HIP HIP HOORAY!

THE END

LOVE THIS POWERPUFF GIRLS ADVENTURE?

Then you'll love the next one EVEN MORE!
In MISSION IMPUFFABLE Blossom,
Bubbles and Buttercup have to stop Pack Rat
from stealing a priceless tiara. When the
tiara's robotic security guard gets involved,
The Powerpuff Girls have a smashing time!

TURN OVER FOR A SNEAK PEEK!

A RUDE
AWAKENING

ZZZZZZ! The Powerpuff Girls were sound asleep in their bed. Don't they look peaceful? It would be such a shame to wake them up ...

BRIIINNNGG!

Buttercup's eyes snapped open. She

switched off the alarm clock on her bedside table. Bouncing out of bed, she flew into the bathroom.

Blossom was still fast asleep. In her dream, she was giving a speech to the United Nations. "And that is how we will achieve world peace," she announced triumphantly. As the audience leapt to its feet to give her a standing ovation, another alarm clock rang.

BRIIIIIIIINNNGG!

Blossom sat up in bed and rubbed her eyes. She squinted at the alarm clock. The display read 6:00 AM.

"That's odd," she said. "I must have set it early by mistake."

She hit the snooze button and went back to sleep.

Next to her, Bubbles was snoring gently

and cuddling Octi, her purple stuffed octopus.

BRIIIIIIIIIIIIINNNGG!

Another alarm clock started ringing.

"Nooo!" groaned Bubbles. "I haven't had enough beauty sleep." She pulled her pillow over her head to block out the alarm.

"Wakey wakey!" shouted Buttercup.

SPLASH!

She tipped a bucket of cold water onto the bed.

"Hey!" squealed Bubbles.

"Yikes!" shrieked Blossom.

They were suddenly wide awake. Bubbles and Blossom jumped out of bed, their wet pyjamas dripping puddles on the rug.

"What gives, Buttercup?" said Blossom, glaring at her sister.

"You slept through the first three alarms," she told them. "So I needed a back-up plan."

Blossom pushed wet hair out of her face. "So you decided to go for the Ice Bucket Challenge?"

"Hey," said Buttercup. "I thought you'd be happy. You're the one who's always saying it's important to have a Plan B!"

Buttercup tossed towels to her shivering sisters. "It didn't just wake you up," she told them. "It also saved time. Now you don't need to take a shower!"

"Why are you in such a hurry this morning?" Bubbles asked. Normally Buttercup had to be dragged out of bed on school days.

"Have you forgotten what today is?" asked Buttercup.

Bubbles thought for a moment. "Is it Unicorn Appreciation Day?"

"Do we have a maths test?" Blossom asked hopefully.

"No," said Buttercup. "It's our school trip to the Townsville Museum!"

"Oh, yeah!" said Blossom. "We're going to have so many learning opportunities today!"

"What are you talking about?" said Buttercup. "School trips mean no work. Whoo hoo!"

"I can't wait to see all the cute animals," said Bubbles. The Townsville Museum had a big natural history section.

"Dude, you know they're dead, right?" said Buttercup.

"I hope we have time to see everything – there's a huge science exhibition and a fascinating local history display," said Blossom.

"It's going to be awesome!" said Buttercup.

Blossom looked at her sister curiously. "I didn't know you were interested in local history, Buttercup."

"I'm not," said Buttercup. "I can't wait to see Fat Mabel."

"It's not nice to call people rude names," said Bubbles.

"A Fat Mabel is a cannon," explained Buttercup. "One of the most powerful in the world. And the Townsville Museum has one!"

The Powerpuff Girls got dressed quickly and went downstairs to breakfast. Professor Utonium was stirring a saucepan of bubbling porridge. He had an apron on over his lab coat.

"You girls are up early today," said the Professor.

"We're going to the Townsville Museum on a school trip," Buttercup told him.

"That sounds very educational," said the Professor approvingly. He scooped porridge into their bowls.

"We don't have time for breakfast," said Buttercup. "We're in a rush."

"Growing girls need to eat a well-balanced breakfast," said Professor Utonium. "It's scientifically proven to be the most important meal of the day."

"We get to see the grand unveiling of the Rainbow Heart Tiara today," said Blossom. "It belonged to Cleopatra."

The ancient Egyptian leader was one of the Powerpuff Girls' heroes.

"Cleopatra kicked butt," said Buttercup.

"And she had great taste in accessories," said Bubbles.

"Ah yes," said the Professor. "The museum asked me to help out with security. I designed a special robot to guard the tiara."

Buttercup had already finished a second helping of porridge. "Could you eat any slower?" she asked her sisters. She gobbled up the last few bites of Bubbles' porridge. "Can we go now?"

Professor Utonium opened up his newspaper. The headline read, *Rodent Robber Raids Retailers.*

"Looks like Pack Rat has been stealing jewellery again," said Blossom.

"That reminds me," gasped Bubbles. "I forgot to put on accessories!"

"We don't have time!" said Buttercup.

"There's always time to accessorize!" replied Bubbles. She flew upstairs to the bedroom. When she came back downstairs, she was wearing a sparkly necklace, a glittery bracelet and several shiny rings.

"NOW can we go?!" said Buttercup impatiently.

"Wait!" cried Blossom. "I need to pack my school supplies!"

Buttercup groaned in frustration. "We're going on a school trip," she said. "You don't need school supplies!"

"I want to take notes on everything we learn at the museum!" said Blossom. She ran upstairs and came back down with a backback bulging with notebooks, pens and highlighters in every shade of the rainbow.

Finally, the Powerpuff Girls made it out of the door. When they reached the end of the path the front door opened again.

"Girls!" called Professor Utonium. "You forgot your packed lunches!" He held up three lunchbags.

Buttercup gasped. She sprinted down the path and grabbed the lunchbags. "That would have been a disaster!"

"Be good at school today!" the professor called as The Powerpuff Girls flew away.

The Powerpuff Girls arrived at school just before the bell rang.

Ms Keane took the register. "Now remember children," she told the class. "I expect you all to be on your best behaviour at the museum. That means no touching the exhibits."

"Awww," moaned Buttercup.

A school bus was waiting outside of the school gates. The children climbed inside. Bubbles and Buttercup sat next to each other.

"Hey, Blossom!" called a dark-haired boy with glasses. "There's a seat next to me!"

Blossom's cheeks blushed as pink as her dress.

"Thanks, Jared," she said, sitting down next to him.

"Blossom and Jared sitting in a tree," sang Buttercup. "K-I-S-S-I-N-G!"

Blossom glared at her sister. "Cut it out, Buttercup!"

The bus started driving to the museum.

Before long, though, it stopped moving forward.

"Come on, come on!" muttered Buttercup. She looked out of the window and saw a long queue of cars.

HONK HONK!

BEEP BEEP!

Read

MISSION IMPUFFABLE

to find out what happens next!

RODENT RUMBLE

Pack Rat is trying to steal the jewels from this maze.
Can you help Buttercup find the fastest route to
collect them all before he takes them?

CALLING ALL PPG FANS!

What's Mojo Jojo's deepest secret?
Which villains are in a book club?
And which episode features a dancing panda?

Dazzle your friends with facts about
The Powerpuff Girls, play quizzes and games and find
out secret information about all your favourite characters in:

THE POWERPUFF GIRLS OFFICIAL HANDBOOK!